A catalogue record for this book is available from the
British Library

Published by Ladybird Books Ltd
27 Wrights Lane London W8 5TZ
A Penguin Company
© LADYBIRD BOOKS LTD MCMXCIX
Stories in this book were previously published
by Ladybird Books Ltd in the *Favourite Tales* series.

MY
LADYBIRD
BOOK OF

10

STORYTIME
TALES

Ladybird

Contents

The Enormous Turnip

based on a traditional folk tale

retold by **Nicola Baxter**

illustrated by **Peter Stevenson**

The Three Billy Goats Gruff

based on a traditional folk tale

retold by **Joan Stimson**

illustrated by **Chris Russell**

The Little Red Hen

based on a traditional folk tale

retold by **Ronne Randall**

illustrated by **Stephen Holmes**

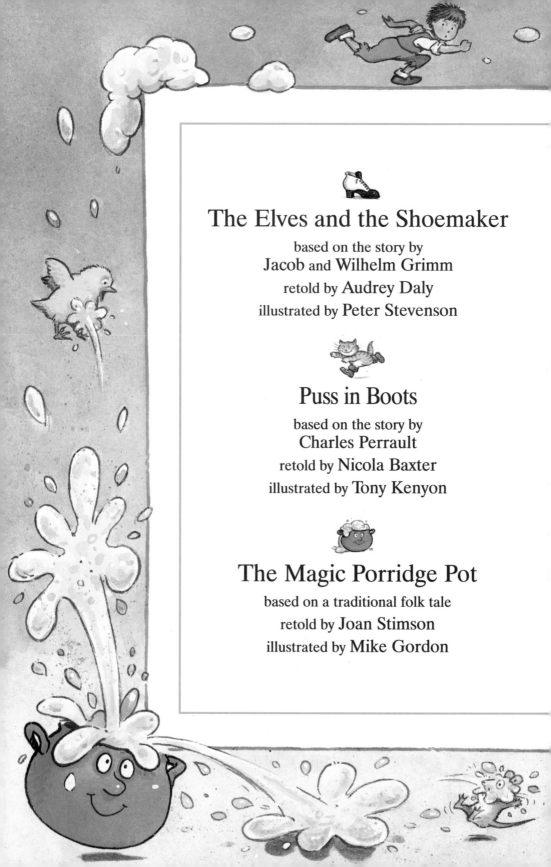

The Elves and the Shoemaker

based on the story by
Jacob and **Wilhelm Grimm**
retold by **Audrey Daly**
illustrated by **Peter Stevenson**

Puss in Boots

based on the story by
Charles Perrault
retold by **Nicola Baxter**
illustrated by **Tony Kenyon**

The Magic Porridge Pot

based on a traditional folk tale
retold by **Joan Stimson**
illustrated by **Mike Gordon**

Chicken Licken

based on a traditional folk tale
retold by **Joan Stimson**
illustrated by **Petula Stone**

Tom Thumb

based on the story by
Jacob and **Wilhelm Grimm**
retold by **Audrey Daly**
illustrated by **Peter Stevenson**

cover and borders illustrated by
Peter Stevenson

The Gingerbread Man

Once upon a time, a little old woman and a little old man lived by themselves in a little old house by the side of a road.

One day, the little old woman decided to make a special treat. "I will make a gingerbread man," she said.

So the little old woman made a
gingerbread man and put him in
the oven to bake. But before long,
she heard a tiny voice calling,
"Let me out! Let me out!"

The little old woman went to the
oven to listen. Then she opened
the oven door.

The gingerbread man jumped
right out! He skipped across the
kitchen and ran straight outside.

The little gingerbread man was on his way down the road before the little old woman and the little old man were out of the house. They couldn't run nearly as fast as he could.

"Stop! We want to eat you. Stop, little gingerbread man!" they cried, quite out of breath.

But the gingerbread man just sang,

> *"Run, run, as fast as you can,*
> *You can't catch me,*
> *I'm the gingerbread man!"*

Soon the gingerbread man met a cow. "Stop, little man!" mooed the cow. "You look very good to eat!"

But the gingerbread man just ran faster. And he sang,

> *"Run, run, as fast as you can,*
> *You can't catch me,*
> *I'm the gingerbread man!"*

The cow ran and ran, but she could not catch the little gingerbread man.

Farther down the road, the gingerbread man met a horse. "Stop, little man!" said the horse. "You look *very* good to eat, and I'm hungry!"

But the gingerbread man just ran faster.

The horse galloped and galloped as fast as he could, but he wasn't fast enough to catch the gingerbread man.

"I have run away from a little old woman, a little old man, and a cow," cried the gingerbread man. And he sang as he ran,

> "Run, run, as fast as you can,
> You can't catch me,
> I'm the gingerbread man!"

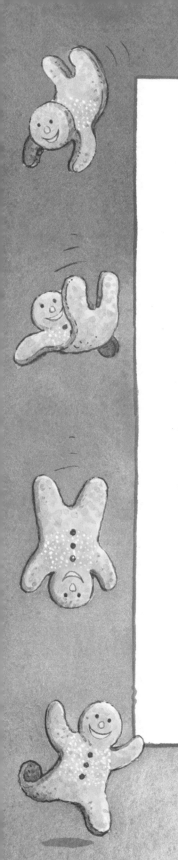

The little gingerbread man ran on
and on, going faster and faster.
He was very proud of his running,
and quite pleased with himself.

At last he met a sly old fox. "Stop!
Stop, little man," said the fox,
grinning and licking his lips. "I
want to talk to you."

But the gingerbread man didn't stop to listen. He just sang,

"Run, run, as fast as you can,
You can't catch me,
I'm the gingerbread man!"

The cunning old fox could run
very fast indeed, and he ran after
the gingerbread man. He followed
him all the way down the path
through the forest.

Before too long they came to a river. The gingerbread man didn't know what to do.

The cunning old fox wasn't far away. "I'll help you," he said, smiling to himself. "If you jump onto my tail, I will take you across. You will be quite safe and dry."

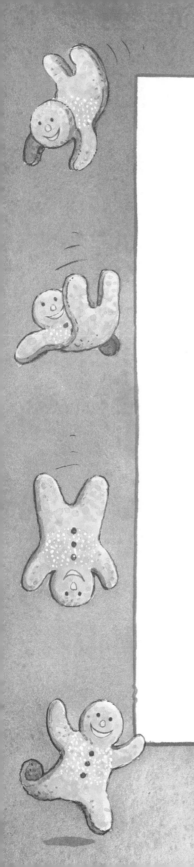

So the little gingerbread man jumped onto the fox's tail and the fox began to swim across the river.

Very soon the fox said, "You are too heavy for my tail. Jump onto my back."

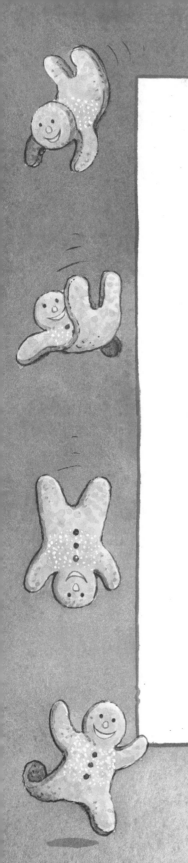

The little gingerbread man
jumped onto the fox's back.

Very soon the fox said, "Little
gingerbread man, you are too
heavy for my back. Why don't you
jump onto my nose?"

And the little gingerbread man
jumped onto the fox's nose.

Finally they reached the other side of the river. The fox threw back his head and tossed the gingerbread man high in the air.

Then *down* fell the gingerbread man, and *snap!* went the old fox.

And that was the end of the little gingerbread man.

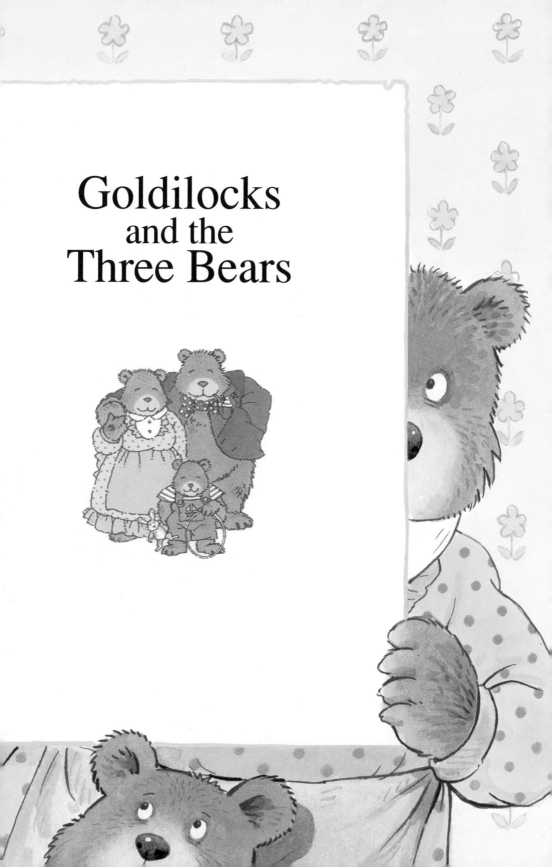

Goldilocks
and the
Three Bears

Once upon a time, there were three bears who lived in a little house right in the middle of the forest.

There was great big Father Bear, and medium-sized Mother Bear, and little tiny Baby Bear.

Honey

One morning, Mother Bear made a big pot of porridge and put it into three bowls for breakfast.

But the porridge was much too hot to eat.

"We will leave it to cool while we go for our early morning walk," said Father Bear. "When we come back, it will be just right." So off they went into the forest.

Nearby there lived a very naughty, mischievous little girl. She was called Goldilocks because she had long, golden hair.

That morning, as she was passing the three bears' house, Goldilocks saw that the front door was open.

"I'll just have a little peep inside," she said to herself.

As soon as she saw the porridge, naughty Goldilocks rushed over to taste it. "I do feel rather hungry," she said.

But the porridge in Father Bear's big bowl was still too hot. And the porridge in Mother Bear's medium-sized bowl was lumpy.

At last Goldilocks tried Baby Bear's porridge. It was just right, so she ate up every spoonful!

After that, Goldilocks decided that she would like to sit down. But Father Bear's big chair was much too high.

Next she sat in Mother Bear's medium-sized chair. "This one is much too hard!" she grumbled.

At last she found Baby Bear's tiny chair. It wasn't too high. It wasn't too hard. It was just right!

Goldilocks leaned back happily in Baby Bear's chair. But she was far too heavy. With a *creak* and a *crack*, the chair fell to pieces.

Bump! Goldilocks landed in a
heap on the floor. "Well, really!"
she said crossly. "I've had such a
shock, I shall have to lie down."

So Goldilocks went upstairs. She tried Father Bear's big bed, but that was far too hard.

And Mother Bear's medium-sized bed was far too soft!

"Now this *is* comfortable," sighed Goldilocks, settling into Baby Bear's little bed. And she fell fast asleep!

Before long, the three bears arrived home from their walk.

"I'm ready for my breakfast *right now,*" said Father Bear. But when he got to the table he cried out in surprise, "Someone's been eating my porridge!"

"And someone's been eating *my* porridge," said Mother Bear. "I wonder why they didn't like it?"

"They must have liked mine!" cried Baby Bear, holding his empty bowl. "Someone's been eating my porridge, and they've eaten it all up!"

"Look!" said Father Bear. "Someone's been sitting in my chair!"

"And someone's been sitting in *my* chair," said Mother Bear.

"Someone's been sitting in my chair," sobbed poor little Baby Bear, "and they've broken it to pieces!"

The three bears began to search the house. Upstairs, Father Bear looked around. "Someone's been sleeping in my bed!" he said.

"And someone's been sleeping in *my* bed," cried Mother Bear.

"Oh!" squeaked Baby Bear. "Someone's been sleeping in my bed and she's *still here!*"

At the sound of Baby Bear's
voice, Goldilocks woke up. The
first thing she saw was Father
Bear, looking very cross.

Goldilocks jumped up in fright. She ran down the stairs and out of the house as fast as she could.

"I don't think she'll trouble us again," said Father Bear, smiling.

And she never did.

The
Enormous
Turnip

One sunny morning a man decided to plant some turnip seeds.

He fetched his fork from the shed and dug a patch of his vegetable garden. It was hard work! He made sure that there were no weeds or big stones.

Then, very carefully, he sprinkled the tiny turnip seeds in a row.

The man took great care of his turnip seeds. Every day, as soon as he woke up, he went down to his vegetable garden and gave them some water.

In only a few days, little green leaves started to appear.

"These are going to be fine turnips," the man said to himself.

The turnips grew very quickly, as turnips do. But one turnip grew faster than all the rest.

Soon it was twice as big as the other turnips. The man was astonished.

"I can almost *see* it growing!" he said proudly.

But the turnip didn't stop. It grew bigger and bigger and bigger until it was… *ENORMOUS!*

One day the man decided that it was time to pull up the enormous turnip.

"We can have it for our dinner," he said to his wife. "I'm sure it will taste as good as it looks!"

So the man took hold of the turnip's huge leaves with both hands and he *pulled*…

and he *pulled*…

and he *pulled* with all his might.

But he couldn't pull up the enormous turnip!

The man called to his wife. "I'm going to need some help with this turnip!" he laughed.

So the man *pulled* the turnip and the woman *pulled* the man. They *pulled* with all their might.

But they couldn't pull up the enormous turnip!

The woman called to a little boy. "Can you come and help us with this enormous turnip?"

So the man *pulled* the turnip and the woman *pulled* the man and the little boy *pulled* the woman. They *pulled* with all their might.

But they couldn't pull up the enormous turnip!

A little girl was walking past. "Please come and help us with this enormous turnip!" called the little boy.

So the man *pulled* the turnip and the woman *pulled* the man and the little boy *pulled* the woman and the little girl *pulled* the little boy. They *pulled* with all their might.

But they couldn't pull up the enormous turnip!

The little girl called to her dog. "Here boy! Come and help us!"

So the man *pulled* the turnip and the woman *pulled* the man and the little boy *pulled* the woman and the little girl *pulled* the little boy and the dog *pulled* the little girl. They *pulled* with all their might.

But they couldn't pull up the enormous turnip!

The dog saw a large orange cat
walking along the fence. "Woof!"
he said. "Come and help us!"

So the man *pulled* the turnip and
the woman *pulled* the man and
the little boy *pulled* the woman
and the little girl *pulled* the little
boy and the dog *pulled* the little
girl and the cat *pulled* the dog.
They *pulled* with all their might.

But they couldn't pull up the
enormous turnip!

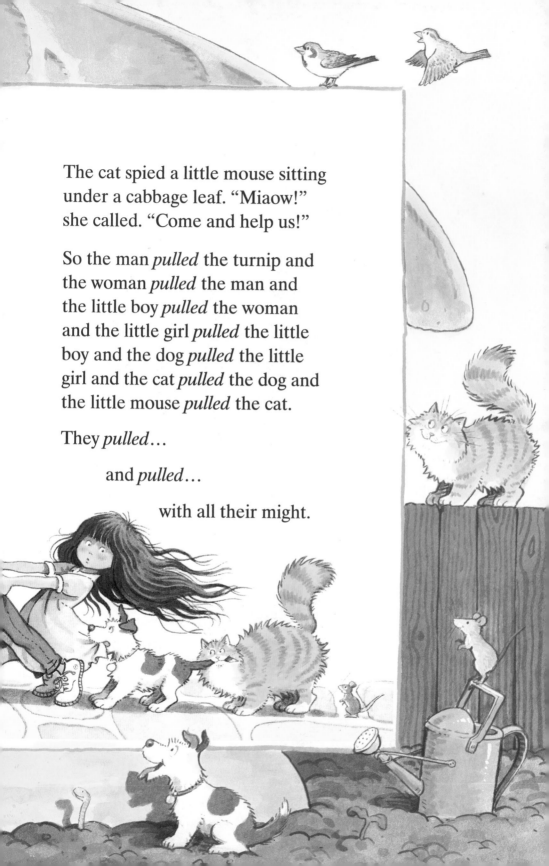

The cat spied a little mouse sitting under a cabbage leaf. "Miaow!" she called. "Come and help us!"

So the man *pulled* the turnip and the woman *pulled* the man and the little boy *pulled* the woman and the little girl *pulled* the little boy and the dog *pulled* the little girl and the cat *pulled* the dog and the little mouse *pulled* the cat.

They *pulled*…

and *pulled*…

with all their might.

"Don't… stop!" panted the man.
"I think… yes, I think… we've
done it!"

And at that the turnip came flying out of the ground. The cat fell on top of the little mouse and the dog fell on top of the cat and the little girl fell on top of the dog and the little boy fell on top of the little girl and the man fell on top of the woman and what fell on top of the man?

The most enormous turnip anyone had ever seen!

When everyone had finished laughing they picked themselves up.

"You must stay and have dinner with us," said the man and his wife to the little boy and the little girl and the dog and the cat and the little mouse.

The turnip was *DELICIOUS!* And you know, it was *so* enormous that they haven't finished eating it yet!

The Three Billy Goats Gruff

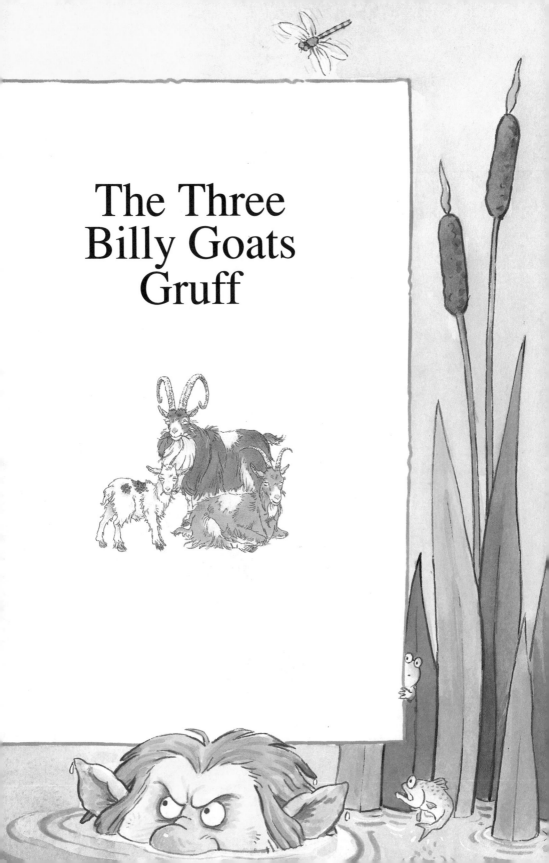

Once upon a time there were
three billy goats called Gruff. One
day, they set off in search of some
sweet, green grass.

Very soon the goats came to a
river. Across the river there was a
meadow, and in the meadow grew
the finest grass that any of them
had ever seen.

Now, there was a wooden bridge over the river, and under this bridge lived a *very* fierce and ugly troll. Every time he heard footsteps going *trip, trap, trip, trap,* across the bridge, he jumped out and gobbled up whoever was trying to cross.

The three billy goats Gruff were very frightened of the troll, but they still longed to eat the sweet, green grass.

After a while the youngest billy goat Gruff stepped forward. "I'm tired of waiting," he said. "I will try to cross the bridge."

Trip, trap, trip, trap, went the little goat's hooves on the wooden planks. Soon he was halfway across.

Suddenly, *up* popped the ugly troll! "Who's that trip-trapping over *my* bridge?" he roared.

"It's only me… the littlest billy goat Gruff," said the frightened goat in a tiny voice. "I'm off to the meadow to eat the green grass."

"Then I'm coming to gobble you up!" roared the troll.

"Oh, *please* don't gobble me up," said the youngest billy goat Gruff. "Wait until the second billy goat Gruff comes along. He's much fatter than I am."

And the youngest billy goat Gruff crossed the bridge and skipped off into the meadow to eat the sweet, green grass.

Then the second billy goat Gruff stepped forward. "Now I will try to cross the bridge," he said.

Trip, trap, trip, trap, went his hooves on the wooden planks. Soon he was halfway across.

Suddenly, *up* popped the ugly troll! "Who's that trip-trapping over *my* bridge?" he roared.

"It's only me… the second billy goat Gruff," said the goat. "I'm off to the meadow to eat the green grass."

"Then I'm going to gobble you up!" roared the troll.

"Oh, *please* don't gobble me up," said the second billy goat Gruff. "Wait until the third billy goat Gruff comes along. He's *very* big and fat!"

And the second billy goat Gruff
crossed the bridge and skipped
off into the meadow to eat the
sweet, green grass.

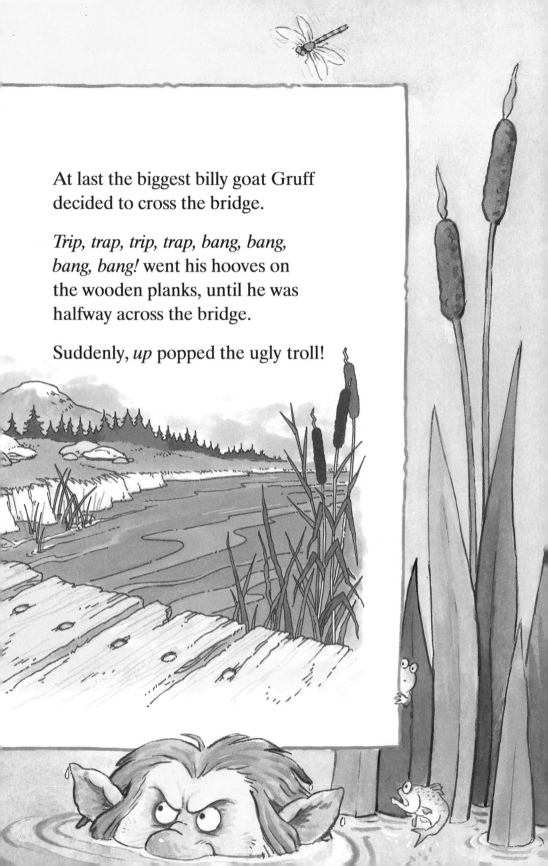

At last the biggest billy goat Gruff
decided to cross the bridge.

*Trip, trap, trip, trap, bang, bang,
bang, bang!* went his hooves on
the wooden planks, until he was
halfway across the bridge.

Suddenly, *up* popped the ugly troll!

"Who's that trip-trapping over *my* bridge?" roared the troll.

"It's me… the biggest billy goat Gruff," said the goat in his loud, gruff voice. "I'm off to the meadow to eat the green grass."

"Then I'm coming to gobble you up!" roared the troll.

"Oh no, you're not!" bellowed the biggest billy goat Gruff. "I'M COMING TO GOBBLE *YOU* UP!"

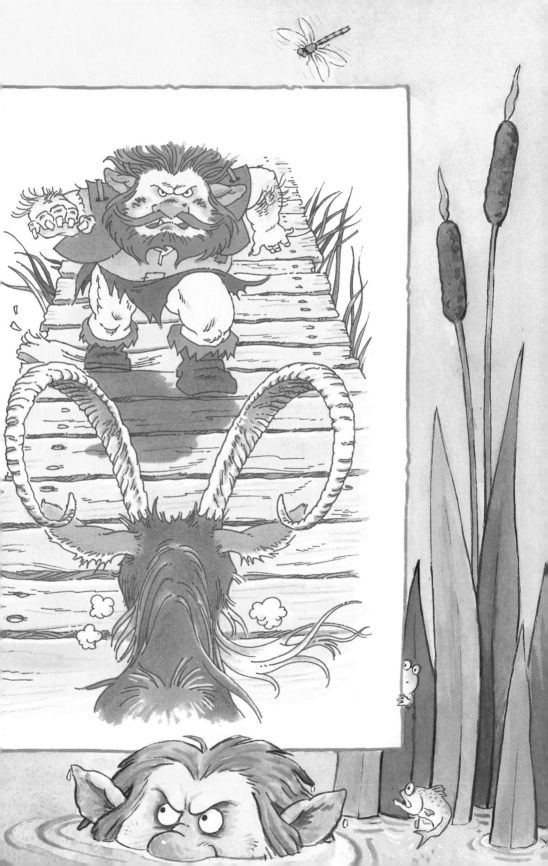

Then the biggest billy goat Gruff lowered his mighty horns and thundered towards the troll. *Trip, trap, trip, trap, bang, bang, BANG, BANG!*

He butted the ugly troll high into the air.

SPLASH! The troll fell down and
down, head first into the deep
water. The river rushed on,
carrying the troll far, far away.

The biggest billy goat Gruff
smiled to himself and skipped off
into the meadow to eat the sweet,
green grass.

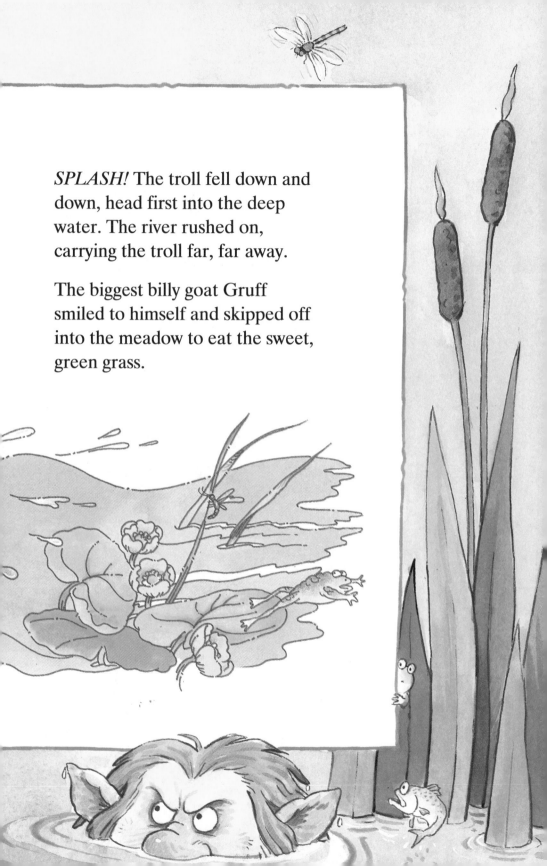

The ugly troll was never seen again. And from that day on, no one was afraid to cross the bridge.

As for the three billy goats Gruff, they all ate so much sweet, green grass that they grew into very fat billy goats indeed!

The Little
Red Hen

Once upon a time there was a little red hen who lived on a farm.

One morning, the little red hen found some grains of wheat. She took them to her friends in the farmyard.

"Who will help me to plant this wheat?" the little red hen asked her friends.

"Not I," said the cat.

"Not I," said the rat.

"Not I," said the pig.

"Then I shall plant the wheat myself,"
said the little red hen.

And that's just what she did. She
planted the grains in a neat row in the
sunniest part of the field.

The little red hen looked after the wheat carefully. She watered it and watched it grow.

At last the wheat was tall and strong and golden. The little red hen knew it was ready to be cut.

"Who will help me to cut the wheat?"
the little red hen asked her friends.

"Not I," said the cat.

"Not I," said the rat.

"Not I," said the pig.

"Then I shall cut the wheat myself,"
said the little red hen.

And that's just what she did. With her
little scythe, she carefully cut down
each stalk of golden wheat.

Then she went back to her friends.
"Who will help me to take
the wheat to the miller?"
she asked.

"Not I," said the cat.

"Not I," said the rat.

"Not I," said the pig.

"Then I shall take the wheat to the miller myself," said the little red hen.

And that's just what she did. She carried the wheat to the mill, and the miller ground it into flour. He put the flour into a sack for the little red hen.

The little red hen took the sack of flour back to the farmyard.

"Who will help me to take this flour to the baker?" she asked her friends.

"Not I," said the cat.

"Not I," said the rat.

"Not I," said the pig.

"Then I shall take it to the baker myself," said the little red hen.

And that's just what she did. The baker made the flour into a loaf of fresh, tasty bread. The little red hen took it back to the farmyard.

"Who will help me to eat this bread?"
the little red hen asked her friends.

"I will!" said the cat.

"I will!" said the rat.

"I will!" said the pig.

"No, you will not!" said the little red hen. "I shall eat this fresh, tasty bread all by myself!"

And that's just what she did!

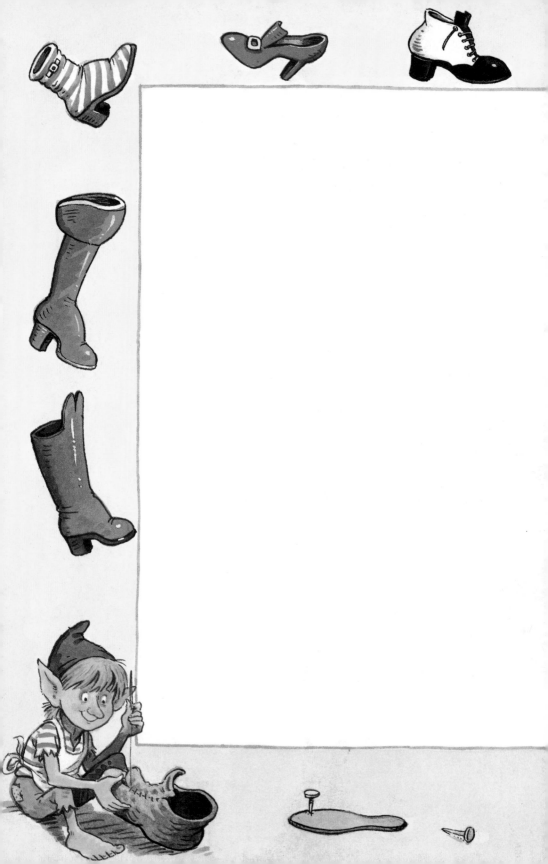

The Elves
and the
Shoemaker

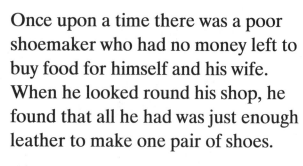

Once upon a time there was a poor shoemaker who had no money left to buy food for himself and his wife. When he looked round his shop, he found that all he had was just enough leather to make one pair of shoes.

As he carefully cut out the shoes, he wondered sadly if anyone would ever come along to buy them. Then he laid out the leather on his workbench, ready to sew the next day, and went upstairs to bed.

In the morning, when he went to his workbench, the shoemaker couldn't believe his eyes. Instead of the leather he had cut out the night before, he saw a pair of fine shoes, already made.

The shoemaker looked carefully at the shoes. The stitches were small and even, and the shoes had been polished until they shone. He was very puzzled and showed them to his wife. Who could have made the shoes so perfectly?

Later that day, a rich woman came into the shop to buy some shoes. When the shoemaker showed her the pair he had found on his workbench, the woman smiled.

"These are very fine shoes," she said as she tried them on. "They fit perfectly. I'll give you five pieces of silver for them."

Now the shoemaker could buy some food, and he could also buy enough leather for *two* pairs of shoes.

As before, he cut out the leather and went to bed.

Once again, the same thing happened.
When the shoemaker went to his
workbench next day, there were two
pairs of fine shoes waiting for him.

They were polished so that they
glowed in the sunlight, and the
stitches were small and even.

That afternoon, a rich merchant came
into the shop. He liked the shoes so
much that he bought *both* pairs, and
he paid the shoemaker well for them.

That day, the shoemaker was able to buy enough leather for *four* pairs of shoes. Just as before, he cut out the leather and left it on his workbench overnight. And in the morning he found four fine pairs of shoes there instead.

The same thing happened night after night. And day after day, rich people came to buy the shoes. Soon the shoemaker and his wife were rich too.

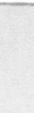

One evening, not long before
Christmas, the shoemaker said to his
wife, "Someone has been helping us
all this time, sewing the shoes so
beautifully, and we still don't know
who it is. How can we find out?"

"Well," said his wife, "why don't we
stay up tonight and watch?"

So after dinner, they lit a candle and
went into the shop. They hid behind
the counter and waited to see what
would happen.

At last the door opened and in ran two tiny elves, dressed in rags. They went straight to the workbench, picked up the leather lying there, and set to work.

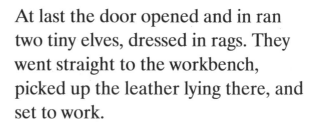

They sewed and hammered until all
the shoes were finished. And they
polished every shoe until it shone in
the moonlight. Then they ran quickly
away.

The next morning, the shoemaker said to his wife, "Those elves have been working so hard for us. How can we ever repay them?"

"I know!" said his wife. "Why don't we make them something warm to wear? Their own clothes were thin and torn, and their little feet were bare. I could start by knitting them little caps, and you could make them some shoes."

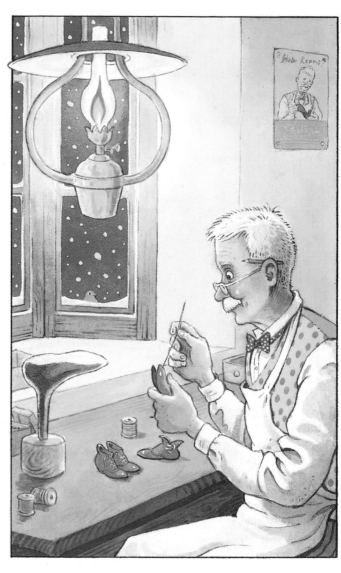

The shoemaker thought that was a very good idea. That evening, he carefully made two pairs of tiny shoes, and his wife knitted two little caps.

Over the next few days, the shoemaker helped his wife to make all sorts of clothes for the elves. They made some little shirts, trousers and waistcoats. Finally, the shoemaker's wife knitted two tiny pairs of socks.

By Christmas Eve, everything stood
ready in a little pile. The shoemaker's
wife fetched some pretty paper and
ribbons, and they wrapped each
present one by one.

The shoemaker was so pleased with
the little shoes he had made that he
saved them till last, and wrapped
them up very carefully.

Then they put all the presents out on
the workbench, and hid behind the
counter to wait for the elves.

In the middle of the night the elves dashed in, ready to start work. But when they went to the workbench, all they found there was the little pile of presents.

The elves looked at each other in surprise. Then they realised that the presents were for them, and they laughed and began to unwrap the packages.

When they saw the clothes, they leapt with joy. They took off all their ragged things and put on their brand new outfits.

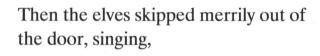

Then the elves skipped merrily out of the door, singing,

"Oh what handsome boys we are!
We will work on shoes no more!"

That was the last the shoemaker and his wife saw of the two little men. But they never forgot the elves, and they were rich and happy for the rest of their lives.

Puss
in Boots

Once upon a time there was a miller who had three sons. When the miller died, he left the mill to his eldest son and a donkey to his second son. They were able to set to work straightaway.

But all that was left for the youngest son was his father's cat.

"Poor Puss," said the miller's son.
"How shall we manage?"

"Don't worry," said the cat. "Give me
a pair of boots and a bag and we will
do very well together."

When the miller's son brought the
things the cat wanted, Puss got ready.
He put on his boots and left the bag,
filled with lettuce leaves, in a field.

Very soon, a little rabbit came to
nibble the lettuce.

Quick as a flash, Puss caught the rabbit in his bag and carried it to the King's palace.

"Your Majesty," said Puss, "please accept this fine rabbit as a present from my master, the Marquis of Carrabas."

"I've never heard of him," said the King, "but you deserve a treat from the kitchen."

The next day, Puss heard that the King and his daughter would be driving by the river.

"Master," he said, "do what I say and we shall be rich. You must take off your clothes and swim in the river. And you must believe that your name is the Marquis of Carrabas."

"I've never heard of him," said the miller's son, "but I'll do as you say, Puss."

Before long, the King drove past with his daughter, the Princess. He was pleased to see Puss again.

"Your Majesty," said Puss, bowing low, "a very terrible thing has happened. My master, the Marquis of Carrabas, was swimming in the river when some thieves came and stole all his clothes!"

"How dreadful!" exclaimed the King and the Princess together.

The King sent off to the palace at once for some clothes. When the miller's son put them on, he looked very handsome.

"Please come and ride in our carriage," said the King. "May I present my daughter?"

Puss ran quickly on ahead. When he saw some men making hay in a field, he shouted to them, "The King is coming. If he asks, you must say that this land belongs to the Marquis of Carrabas."

"We've never heard of him," said the haymakers, "but we'll do as you say."

Soon the King drove past in his carriage with the Princess and the miller's son. "Tell me, my man," said the King to a haymaker, "whose land is this?"

"It belongs to the Marquis of Carrabas, Your Majesty," the man replied at once.

Meanwhile, Puss had found out that
the land was really owned by an ogre
who lived in a huge castle nearby.

Puss quickly made his way to the
castle and knocked on the door.
"Sir, is it true that you are a very
good magician?" he asked the ogre.

The ogre, who liked to show off, replied, "Yes, it's true. I can even turn myself into a lion!"

Quick as a flash, the ogre became a fierce, roaring lion!

Puss was so startled that he scrambled
to the top of a chest of drawers to
hide.

When the ogre had changed himself back again, Puss jumped down. "Turning into a lion must be easy for someone as big and strong as you," he said. "But can you turn yourself into something *tiny* – like a mouse?"

"Of course I can!" roared the ogre. "Just watch!"

In the blink of an eye, the ogre
became a little mouse scurrying across
the floor. Puss instantly
pounced on him and
ate him up.

"Now that the ogre is gone," Puss said
to himself, "this castle will make a
very fine home for my master, the
Marquis of Carrabas."

The King was most impressed by the handsome young man who owned such rich land and lived in such a magnificent castle. "He would make a fine husband for my daughter," the King said.

So the miller's son and the Princess and Puss lived happily ever after. And now *everyone* has heard of the Marquis of Carrabas!

The Magic
Porridge Pot

Once upon a time, there was a little girl who lived with her widowed mother. They were very poor, and one day they had nothing left to eat at all.

The little girl was so hungry that she ran into the woods and began to cry.

"Whatever is the matter?" asked a kind voice.

The kind voice belonged to an old woman. When she heard how hungry the little girl was, she gave her a magic cooking pot.

"Just say the words, 'Cook, little pot, cook!'" she explained, "and it will give you lovely, hot porridge.

"But once the porridge is cooked, you must say, 'Stop, little pot, stop!'"

The little girl spoke to the pot right away. "Cook, little pot, cook!" she said, and to her surprise, it began to bubble!

The porridge smelled wonderful. As soon as it was cooked, the little girl said, "Stop, little pot, stop!"

Then she ate up every last bit!

The little girl ran all the way home. She showed her mother the magic cooking pot and told her what the old woman had said.

Her mother was delighted.

"All our troubles are over," she cried.

And she was right. Because, whenever the little girl and her mother were hungry, all they had to say was, "Cook, little pot, cook!"

Each time, the magic pot would cook them some lovely, hot porridge.

The little girl and her mother could hardly believe how lucky they were.

One day the little girl went out for a walk. While she was away, her mother felt hungry, so she picked up the magic pot.

"Cook, little pot, cook!" she said, and the pot set to work. The mother was soon so busy eating that she forgot to tell the pot to stop!

On and on cooked the pot. Soon the porridge began to spill over the top.

As soon as the mother saw what was happening, she knew that she must tell the pot to stop cooking.

But she had forgotten the words!

On and on cooked the magic pot. First the porridge covered the kitchen table. Then it spread across the floor. Soon the *whole house* was full of porridge.

The porridge spilled into the street and filled all the other houses. Then it began to ooze along other streets.

And still the magic pot went on cooking!

FOR SALE

By now the town was beginning to *drown* in porridge. The people started to panic. They ran out of their porridge-filled houses and into the porridge-filled streets.

"Help!" cried the mother. "I must stop the magic cooking pot, but I can't remember the words."

"Help!" cried the townspeople. "Soon the whole *world* will be filled with porridge!"

Just as the porridge reached the last house in the town, the little girl came back from her walk. She could hardly believe her eyes.

"*Please* tell the magic pot to stop making porridge," begged her mother.

The little girl took hold of the magic pot and said sternly, "Stop, little pot, STOP!"

And, at last, the magic pot stopped cooking porridge.

The whole town breathed a sigh of relief. It hadn't drowned in porridge after all.

But, if ever you visit there, be prepared… for porridge, porridge and *more porridge*!

TONI'S
MENU
LARGE PORRIDGE
2.00
SMALL PORRIDGE
1.00
MED PORRIDGE
1.50
EXTRAS...
BOWL 10p SPOON 5p

Chicken
Licken

Once upon a time there was a little chick called Chicken Licken.

One day, as he was playing, an acorn fell on his head.

"Help!" thought Chicken Licken. "The sky is falling down!"

And he ran off to tell the King.

On the way, Chicken Licken met Henny Penny.

"Oh! Henny Penny!" cried Chicken Licken. "The sky is falling down and I'm off to tell the King."

"Then I shall come too," said Henny Penny.

So Chicken Licken and Henny Penny hurried off to find the King.

On the way, Chicken Licken and Henny Penny met Cocky Locky.

"Oh! Cocky Locky!" cried Chicken Licken. "The sky is falling down and we're off to tell the King."

"Then I shall come too," said Cocky Locky.

So Chicken Licken, Henny Penny and Cocky Locky hurried off to find the King.

On the way, Chicken Licken, Henny Penny and Cocky Locky met Ducky Lucky.

"Oh! Ducky Lucky!" cried Chicken Licken. "The sky is falling down and we're off to tell the King."

"Then I shall come too," said Ducky Lucky.

So Chicken Licken, Henny Penny,
Cocky Locky and Ducky Lucky
hurried off to find the King.

On the way, Chicken Licken, Henny Penny, Cocky Locky and Ducky Lucky met Drakey Lakey.

"Oh! Drakey Lakey!" cried Chicken Licken. "The sky is falling down and we're off to tell the King."

"Then I shall come too," said Drakey Lakey.

So Chicken Licken, Henny Penny, Cocky Locky, Ducky Lucky and Drakey Lakey hurried off to find the King.

On the way, Chicken Licken, Henny Penny, Cocky Locky, Ducky Lucky and Drakey Lakey met Goosey Loosey.

"Oh! Goosey Loosey!" cried Chicken Licken. "The sky is falling down and we're off to tell the King."

"Then I shall come too," said Goosey Loosey.

So Chicken Licken, Henny Penny,
Cocky Locky, Ducky Lucky, Drakey
Lakey and Goosey Loosey hurried off
to find the King.

On the way, Chicken Licken, Henny Penny, Cocky Locky, Ducky Lucky, Drakey Lakey and Goosey Loosey met Turkey Lurkey.

"Oh! Turkey Lurkey!" cried Chicken Licken. "The sky is falling down and we're off to tell the King."

"Then I shall come too," said Turkey Lurkey.

So Chicken Licken, Henny Penny,
Cocky Locky, Ducky Lucky, Drakey
Lakey, Goosey Loosey and Turkey
Lurkey hurried off to find the King.

But on the way, they met Foxy Loxy!

"Good morning," said Foxy Loxy. "Where are you all going in such a hurry?"

"Oh! Foxy Loxy!" cried Chicken Licken. "The sky is falling down and we're off to tell the King."

"Follow me," said Foxy Loxy. "I know just where to find the King."

So Chicken Licken, Henny Penny, Cocky Locky, Ducky Lucky, Drakey Lakey, Goosey Loosey and Turkey Lurkey all followed Foxy Loxy.

But he didn't take them to the King.
He led them straight to his den,
where his wife and all the little foxes
were waiting for their dinner.

Then the foxes ate up Chicken Licken, Henny Penny, Cocky Locky, Ducky Lucky, Drakey Lakey, Goosey Loosey and Turkey Lurkey.

And Chicken Licken never did find the King to tell him that the sky was falling down!

Tom
Thumb

There was once a woodsman and
his wife who were very sad
because they had no children.

"If only we had a child to love,"
said the wife, "I wouldn't mind if
he were as small as my thumb!"

Time passed and at last they had
a son, which made them both very
happy.

Strangely enough, the boy never
grew any bigger than a man's
thumb, and so they called him
"Tom Thumb".

One day, as Tom's father set off for work, he sighed, "If only Tom were bigger, he could drive the cart into the forest for me."

Tom looked at his mother. "I can do it anyway!" he said. "If you will harness the horse, Mother, I'll show you how." Tom's mother did as he asked.

"Now put me in the horse's ear," said Tom. "I'll tell him which way to go."

So off went the cart with Tom tucked in the horse's ear. When Tom said, "Turn left," or "Turn right," the horse did just that.

Two men, who were walking in the forest, were surprised to see a horse and cart going along without a driver. They followed the cart to see where it went.

When the cart stopped, the two men were amazed to see Tom's father lift him down from the horse's ear.

"What a clever little fellow that is," said one of the men. "Will you sell him to us?"

"I would never sell him," said the woodsman proudly. "He is my son."

But Tom whispered, "Go on, Father, let me go with them. It will be an adventure, and I know I can get home soon."

The woodsman didn't want to, but at last he sold Tom for a lot of money.

One of the men put Tom in his pocket, saying, "We can put him on show in the towns. He is going to make us rich!" Then they set off.

Towards evening, Tom called out,
"Please put me down so that I can
stretch my legs."

When the men put him down,
Tom ran straight off and hid. The
men looked everywhere, but he
had disappeared.

Tom looked for somewhere safe
to sleep. He soon found an empty
snail shell and curled up inside it.
Just as he was falling asleep, he
heard voices nearby.

Two thieves were talking. "We'll
sneak into the parson's house and
steal his money!" said one.

"Take me with you," said Tom in a
loud voice. "I can help you!"

The men were puzzled. They could
hear a voice, but they couldn't see
anyone. They were astonished
when they found the tiny boy.

"I can get in through a crack in the window," said Tom, "and I can throw the money down to you."

The men agreed to take Tom with them and see what he could do.

When they got to the parson's house, Tom did as he had said. Then, standing on the window ledge, he shouted, "Do you want *all* the money that's here?"

"Sssh!" said the thieves, frightened. "You'll wake the whole house!"

But Tom shouted even louder.
"HOW MUCH MONEY
SHOULD I THROW DOWN?"

The noise woke the cook, who
was sleeping in the next room.

While the cook got up
to look around, Tom
ran off to the
barn. There
he settled
down to sleep
in the hay.

By the time the cook got
downstairs, the thieves had run
away and there was no sign of
Tom at all.

Next morning the cook went to milk and feed the cow. She picked up the very bundle of hay that Tom was sleeping in.

Tom woke up to find himself being tossed up and down in the cow's mouth. He landed in the cow's stomach with all the hay.

"Stop eating!" yelled Tom. "I'm getting smothered!"

The cook was so startled to hear a voice coming from the cow's mouth that she ran to the parson. "Help!" she cried. "The cow's talking!"

"Don't be silly," said the parson. "Cows don't talk."

Just then Tom shouted again – the parson was astonished.

As soon as he could, Tom crawled out of the cow's stomach and slipped away. No one saw him go.

But Tom's troubles were far from over. A hungry wolf was passing by and saw Tom in the farmyard.

"This will make
a tasty little snack,"
thought the wolf, and he
swallowed Tom in one gulp.

Clever Tom quickly thought of a plan. "Wolf," he called, "if you are still hungry, I know where there is lots of food." And he told the wolf how to get to his very own house, which was not far away.

When they got there, Tom said, "Just crawl through the drain and you'll be in the kitchen, where there is always plenty to eat."

The drain was quite small, but the wolf squeezed and pushed and *just* managed to get through.

In the kitchen, the wolf ate so much that when he tried to crawl back through the drain, he was much too fat!

Then Tom began to shout and sing at the top of his voice.

His parents came to the kitchen
door to see what all the noise was
about.

"It's a wolf!" said Tom's father.
"Where's my axe?"

"Wait, Father!" shouted Tom.
"It's me! I'm here, inside the
wolf's stomach!"

"Tom!" cried his father. "Don't worry, we'll save you!"

Tom's father picked up his axe and hit the wolf over the head. Then, very carefully, he cut a little hole in the wolf's stomach.

Out jumped Tom, safe and sound. "I told you I'd be back soon, Father!" he laughed.

Tom's parents were overjoyed to see him. "We'll never part with you again," said his father, "not for all the money in the world."

"And I will never leave home again," promised Tom. "I've had enough adventures to last a lifetime!"

NIM AT SEA

Also by Wendy Orr

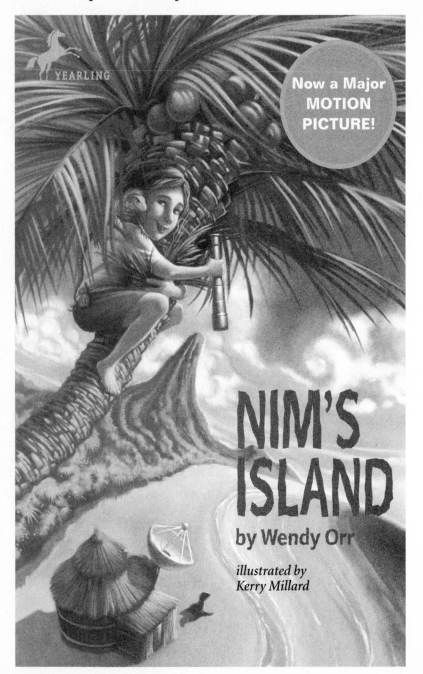

YEARLING

Now a Major
MOTION
PICTURE!

NIM'S
ISLAND

by Wendy Orr

*illustrated by
Kerry Millard*

WENDY ORR
NIM AT SEA

Illustrated by
KERRY MILLARD

Alfred A. Knopf
NEW YORK

THIS IS A BORZOI BOOK PUBLISHED BY ALFRED A. KNOPF

Published in the United States by Alfred A. Knopf, an imprint of Random House Children's Books, a division of
Random House, Inc., New York. Originally published in Australia by Allen & Unwin in 2007.

www.randomhouse.com/kids

Educators and librarians, for a variety of teaching tools, visit us at www.randomhouse.com/teachers

Library of Congress Cataloging-in-Publication Data is available upon request.
ISBN 978-0-440-42232-7 (trade)—ISBN 978-0-385-90535-0 (lib. bdg.)

Printed in the United States of America
March 2008
10 9 8 7 6 5 4 3 2 1
First American Edition

For Paula, who believed in Nim

Prologue

LONG AGO, when Nim was a baby, she'd had both a mother and a dad. Then one day, her mother had decided to investigate the contents of a blue whale's stomach. It was an interesting experiment that no one had done for thousands of years, and Nim's dad, Jack, said that it would have been all right, it should have been safe—but the Troppo Tourists came to make a film of it, shouting and racing their huge pink-and-purple boat around Nim's mother and the whale. The whale panicked and dived so deep that no one ever knew where or when he came back up again.

Nim's mother never came back up at all.

So Jack packed his baby onto his boat and sailed round and round the world—and finally, when the baby had grown into a very little girl, he found the perfect island where he could do his science and Nim could grow, wild and free like the animals they lived with.

The island has white-shell beaches, pale gold sand, and tumbled black rocks. It has a fiery mountain with green rainforest on the high slopes and grasslands at the bottom. There is a pool of fresh water to drink, a waterfall to slide down, and the hut that Jack built in a hidden hollow where the grasslands meet the beach. And around it, there's a maze of reef guarding the island from everything but the smallest boats, so Jack knows the Troppo Tourists or anyone else can never find their island.

But one day, Jack and his boat got lost in a storm—and Nim was left alone on the island, until her e-mail friend Alex Rover, the most famous and cowardly adventure writer in

the whole world, crossed the sea to rescue her. And then
Nim's most secret wish came true: Jack came floating back—
and Alex stayed.

1

IN A PALM TREE, on an island, in the middle of the wide blue sea, is a girl.

Nim's hair is wild, her eyes are bright, and around her neck she wears three cords. One is for a spyglass, one is for a whorly, whistling shell, and the other holds a fat red pocketknife in a sheath.

With the spyglass at her eye, Nim watched the little red seaplane depart. It sailed out through the reef to the deeper dark ocean, bumping across the waves till it was tossed into the bright blue sky. Then it rose so high and so far it was nothing but a speck, and floated out of sight.

"Alex is gone," Nim told Fred.

Fred stared at the coconuts clustered on the trunk.

Fred is an iguana, spiky as a dragon, with a cheerful snub nose. He was sitting on Nim's shoulder, and he cared more about coconuts than he did about saying goodbye. (Marine iguanas don't eat coconut, but no one has ever told Fred.)

As Nim threw three ripe coconuts *thump!* into the sand, she remembered Alex saying, "I never knew anything could taste better than coffee!" the first time Nim opened a coconut for her.

Nim looked down at her father, sitting like a stone on Selkie's Rock. Jack's head was bowed and his shoulders slumped. Nim had never seen him look so sad.

And suddenly she knew she'd made a terrible, terrible mistake.

The mistake began when she answered Alex's very first e-mail, back when she'd thought that the famous Alex Rover was a man and a brave adventurer like the hero in the books "he" wrote. That led to Alex's ending up on the island—and when she did, Jack and Nim wanted her never to leave. Sometimes it felt good to be three instead of two.

But other times Nim wanted Jack just for herself, the way it used to be. Or she wanted Alex just for herself, because Alex was *her* friend before she was Jack's. Sometimes, when Alex and Jack told Nim to go to sleep while they talked late into the night, Nim felt left out and lonely.

Then, earlier this morning, the little red seaplane had arrived, bringing all the things that Alex had asked her editor back in the city to send. It was the first time a plane had ever landed on Nim's island. Nim could tell that Jack was worried that the pilot would notice how beautiful the island was and would want to come back again and again.

Whenever Jack was worried, Nim was too. And when Nim was worried, so were her friends Selkie and Fred. (Selkie is a sea lion who sometimes forgets that Nim is a girl and not a little sea lion pup to be looked after and *whuffled* over.) They both stuck close to Nim every time she walked back and forth between the plane and the hut.

"I've never seen animals do that before!" exclaimed the pilot.

Nim didn't know what to say, partly because she didn't know exactly what he hadn't seen before, and partly because she'd never spoken to any person besides Jack and Alex. She grabbed a crate and opened it up. Inside there were books! Thin books and fat, short books and tall, history and science books, mysteries, adventures, and more and more and more! Nim started to look through one when—

"Come on, Nim!" said Alex. "There'll be time to read when everything's off the plane."

The pilot pulled out two big solar panels. "Great!" Jack exclaimed, because he wanted them for the new room he planned to add to the hut—one created especially for Alex to write her books in. Jack balanced the panels on his head and walked very slowly and carefully up toward the hut.

"Who's going to take this one?" the pilot asked, pointing to a crate.

Nim stepped forward eagerly. But just as she was about to

reach for the crate, the pilot handed it to Alex. First Alex stumbled, then she tripped, then *crash!* the crate fell with a tinkle of broken glass.

"Oh, *no!*" Alex wailed. "What have I done?"

"Jack's test tubes!" Nim shouted. "You should have let me take it!"

"I was trying to help!"

"But I didn't need help! You just got in the way!"

"I'm always in the way these days!" Alex snapped. "Maybe you and Jack would be better off without me."

"I think we would!" Nim shouted, and stomped off without waiting for an answer.

She's right! Alex thought. *Nim and Jack lived here perfectly happily all those years without anyone else—they don't really need me. Nim's been cross with me a lot lately and I've never seen Jack be so worried. I think . . . I think I'm changing their lives too much. What if they've secretly been wanting their old lives back— and just haven't wanted to say so?*

Alex understood about being afraid to say so. Before she came to the island, she was so afraid of saying anything to anyone that she hardly ever left her apartment. She was a famous person, but only through her books. Her life had totally changed since she flew across the world to find Nim.

"Last one!" The pilot handed her a large envelope. "And now, time for me to go."